HAZARD

Also by Frances O'Roark Dowell

Frances O'Roark Dowell

HAZARD

A CAITLYN DLOUHY BOOK

ATHENEUM BOOKS FOR YOUNG READERS

New York London Toronto Sydney New Delhi

For Kate Daniels
In memory of Sam Macdonald

atheneum

Atheneum Books for Young Readers An imprint of Simon & Schuster Children's Publishing Division • 1230 Avenue of the Americas, New York, New York 10020 • This book is a work of fiction. Any references to historical events, real people, or real places are used fictitiously. Other names, characters, places, and events are products of the author's imagination, and any resemblance to actual events or places or persons, living or dead, is entirely coincidental. • Text © 2022 by Frances O'Roark Dowell • Jacket illustration © 2022 by Violet Tobacco • Jacket design by Debra Sfetsios-Conover © 2022 by Simon & Schuster, Inc. • All rights reserved, including the right of reproduction in whole or in part in any form. • ATHENEUM BOOKS FOR YOUNG READERS is a registered trademark of Simon & Schuster, Inc. Atheneum logo is a trademark of Simon & Schuster, Inc. • For information about special discounts for bulk purchases, please contact Simon & Schuster Special Sales at 1-866-506-1949 or business@simonandschuster.com. • The Simon & Schuster Speakers Bureau can bring authors to your live event. For more information or to book an event, contact the Simon & Schuster Speakers Bureau at 1-866-248-3049 or visit our website at www.simonspeakers. com. • Interior design by Irene Metaxatos • The text for this book was set in Bembo Std and Helvetica Neue. • Manufactured in the United States of America • 0422 FFG • First Edition • 10 9 8 7 6 5 4 3 2 1 • Library of Congress Cataloging-in-Publication Data • Names: Dowell, Frances O'Roark, author. • Title: Hazard / Frances O'Roark Dowell. • Description: First edition. | New York : Atheneum Books for Young Readers, 2022. | Audience: Ages 9-13. | Audience: Grades 4-6. | Summary: Told in a series of reports to his therapist, Hazard is resentful about being forced into counseling after being suspended from his school football team for unsportsmanlike conduct, angry that his father has served four tours of duty in Iraq and Afghanistan, angry that his father has lost a leg when an IED blew up—but as his therapy progresses he begins to process what has happened to him and his family, including his father's psychological trauma that has made him refuse to see his sons. • Identifiers: LCCN 2021034200 (print) | LCCN 2021034201 (ebook) | ISBN 9781481424660 (hardcover) | ISBN 9781481424677 (paperback) | ISBN 9781481424684 (ebook) • Subjects: LCSH: Families of military personnel—Juvenile fiction. | Post-traumatic stress disorder—Juvenile fiction. | Fathers and sons—Juvenile fiction. | Anger—Juvenile fiction. | Psychoanalytic counseling— Juvenile fiction. | Amputees—Juvenile fiction. | Afghan War, 2001-—Juvenile fiction. | CYAC: Children of military personnel—Fiction. | Post-traumatic stress disorder—Fiction. | Fathers and sons—Fiction. | Anger—Fiction. | Psychotherapy—Fiction. | Amputees— Fiction. | People with disabilities—Fiction. | Afghan War, 2001-—Fiction. • Classification: LCC PZ7.D75455 Haz 2022 (print) | LCC PZ7.D75455 (ebook) | DDC 813.6 [Fic]—dc23 • LC record available at https://lccn.loc.gov/2021034200 • LC ebook record available at https://lccn.loc.gov/2021034201

And if the body does not do fully as much as the soul?
And if the body were not the soul, what is the soul?

—Walt Whitman
"I Sing the Body Electric"

To begin:
A text from Haz to Jax

J
Jackson >
Sun, Sept 20, 2:14 PM

What up Jax

What up

Check it out

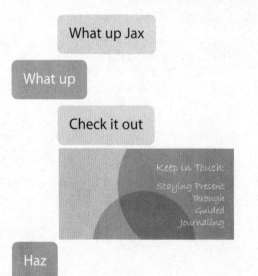

Keep in Touch:
Staying Present
Through
Guided
Journaling

Haz

Dude

What tha

It's a workbook I gotta do cuz like I'm 6

Good times bro

It gets better

Begin at the Beginning

Was there a particular event or situation that caused you to seek therapy?

Sucks to be you

Dude you have no idea

Delivered

To: BarthWB@childrenscounselingservices.com
From: StokesHP@ccs.k12.nc.us
Date: September 21, 8:04 AM
Subject: Assignments

Dear Dr. Barth:

Workbook assignments attached.
See you this afternoon at 4.

Haz

P.S. Are you sure this workbook is basic enough?
Maybe they could add a few more pix
of kids chewing on their pencils
and looking all thoughtful and crap.
Those were friggin' awesome!

Attachment: WorkbookQuestions1-2.docx

Workbook: Keep in Touch: Staying Present Through Guided
Journaling

Q: *Was there a particular event or situation that caused you
to seek therapy?*

The real story is this: the hit was clean.
I know what Coach *thought* he saw,
but he caught it from the wrong angle.
Besides, some refs will throw a flag
just cuz they're bored—
anybody'll tell you that.
And, dude, I didn't "seek" therapy.
Don't put words in my mouth
you'd never hear me say.

Q: *How do you feel about being in therapy?*

Like it's a waste of time.
Like if we're going to do this thing,
let's get it done. Twelve weeks?
Not gonna happen, son.
Coach said I had to do this,
but he didn't say jack about three months.
I'll give you *one*—that puts me back
on the field by October 20.
Come on, dude, chill.
I'll write in your workbook,
I'll "map out the facts" that help
"pull the story together,"
just like you said.
I'll do it fast and I'll do it right.
I'll write you a whole damn book.
But no way I'm calling you Walter,
no matter how many times you ask.

To: BarthWB@childrenscounselingservices.com
From: StokesHP@ccs.k12.nc.us
Date: September 23, 9:02 PM
Subject: It Goes Both Ways

Dear Dr. Barth:

I looked you up.
I mean, if you're gonna know everything
about me, then I ought to know
at least a thing or two about you.
You went to East Carolina? I guess that's okay,
but dude:
you kinda overdid it with the degrees.
You got three sets of letters after your name—
BA, MS, PhD—
and you spend your life talking to kids?
Seems like a waste of an education to me.
But what do I know?
I'm not even in high school yet—
next year, if they let me in after all this crap.
Don't get me wrong: I'm not dumb.
I make mostly As and Bs,
a C here and there
so I don't look like I'm showing off.
I'll probably go to college on a scholarship—
football, that is.

You ever go to games when you were a Pirate?
On your page, it says you graduated college in 2003.
Dude. That's the year East Carolina was 1–11.
That's just sad.
I bet you walked around campus
with your head
hung low.
Maybe *that's* why you do what you do.
You've been through some bad times yourself.
Me, I'm up and running and ready to go.
Catch me if you can, Mr. Pirate Man.

Haz

P.S. You gotta admit I'm good with the lines.
Surprised you, am I right?
No lie, there's more to me
than pads and cleats.
You might *think* you've got me figured out,
but dude: you don't.

To: BarthWB@childrenscounselingservices.com
From: StokesHP@ccs.k12.nc.us
Date: September 24, 4:36 PM
Subject: Workbook Assignment

Dear Dr. Barth:

What'd I tell you?
I came to play.
Questions 3 & 4, completed and good to go.
Document attached and all that.

Haz

Attachment: WorkbookQuestions3-4.docx

Q: *Is there a story behind your name?*

You oughta get my mom to tell it.
She could go on for hours
about how two E-4s on their way to war
took a detour to Hazard, Kentucky,
to get as far away from the army
as they could for a day.
They drove 280 miles from base to a place
with a name that made my mom laugh.
She said her whole *life* had been hazardous up till then.

She downed the daily special and I fell in love
is how my dad told it,
and me and Ty would fake heave every time.
But it wasn't that bad, not really,
knowing your mom and dad took leave
to drive three hundred miles across a state
just to eat chicken-fried steak and tell dumb jokes
two days before they deployed to Iraq.
They got married three months after they got back,
and I showed up nine months after that.

My full and complete name is Hazard Pay Stokes,
and I guess you could call it kind of a joke,

but I like it okay.
Means something extra you get for taking a risk,
the way my mom and dad did, two strangers
out for a ride
across one countryside,
and then the next.
And now one more, I guess.
Only this one don't have a name or a map.
Sometimes I think they're not ever coming back.

Q: *Write about an early experience with one of your parents.*

This one time my dad emailed me
a list of birds he might see
through his barracks window at Camp Taji.
I was this little first-grader freak
who didn't even know they *had* birds in Iraq,
like I thought birds were an American thing.

Anyway, I memorized all the names
just to make him proud the next time we skyped.
Jacksnipe, great snipe, lesser gray shrike,
whiskered tern, whimbrel, collared pratincole,
little bittern, crested lark, red-necked grebe.
I could say the whole list in ten seconds flat.

By the time it was time for my dad to come home,
he'd spotted five of the nine.
Eight months later, he was gone again.
I figured the army sent him to Kandahar
to look for more birds. I figured the word *deploy*
meant *when your father flies away.*

To: WBarth@childrenscounselingservices.com
From: StokesHP@ccs.k12.nc.us
Date: September 25, 3:35 PM
Subject: Re: Vocabulary Help

Dear Dr. Barth:
You know, you could just look up
these words yourself.
But if it gets me through this faster, fine.
You will find a vocabulary lesson attached.
In fact, I'm happy to school you
whenever necessary.

Haz

Attachment: Vocab1.docx

Dr. B's First Vocabulary Lesson: **Deploy**

Definition:

Verb that means to send soldiers from their home base
to a different location, sometimes to a combat zone,
but not always. Most times you're deployed six months
to a year, and you can get deployed over and over. It's
just part of the job.

Use in a sentence:

My mom was deployed once to Iraq before she got out
  of the army.

My dad has been deployed four times:
twice to Iraq, twice to Afghanistan.
Five times if you count Walter Reed Medical Center
  in Bethesda, Maryland,
which my mom counts. My mom counts everything—

Hours it takes to drive from the hospital to home

Minutes it takes us to reply to her texts

Complaints my granny makes about the noise
two boys make in her once-upon-a-time-noiseless house

Days she's been out of work so she can sit
by my dad's hospital bed and listen to him
not talk

To: WBarth@childrenscounselingservices.com
From: StokesHP@ccs.k12.nc.us
Date: September 25, 7:16 PM
Subject: Medical Note

Dear Dr. Barth:

I've been limping around
school for two weeks now, pretending
I got a pulled hamstring.
But a pulled hamstring
don't last forever.
So what do I say until we're done here?
(Hope you got that October 20 deadline
down on your calendar.)

Maybe you could write me a note
that says I've got to take it easy
a few more weeks,
that it's not just my hamstring
but a hip pointer too?
Nobody'll ask to see the bruise.
You're not that kind of doc,
but who's gonna know?
Just give me something to show
anyone who asks why
I'm not playing or at practice.

I know you'll probably say
I should tell them the truth.
Not gonna happen.
I got a rep to protect—not just on my team,
but across the division.
Every receiver, every tight end,
anybody going out for a pass
needs to fear me.
If the ball's coming your way, so am I.
I'm the best safety my age in Cumberland County.
Bet you didn't know that.

My opponents can't be thinking I'm weak.
They won't know this is just a step
I gotta take if I want to get back on the field.
Give me some help here, dude.
You want me to talk?
Write me a hall pass.
Give me a way out.

Haz

P.S. More workbook input.
Attached, per usual.

Attachment: WorkbookQuestion5.docx

Q: *Write about a favorite family activity.*

Dude, can we discuss the fact that I'm not five?
There's gotta be a better workbook out there,
maybe one that asks questions like,
What was the best prank you and Jackson pulled
in seventh grade? (No contest: the time
we got to Mr. Hermann's class early
and superglued twenty UNC Fathead decals
on the ceiling—
the guy hated Carolina like nobody's business.)

I mean, I've got some interesting material to share,
and all this book wants me to talk about
is how my family played checkers or something.

Okay whatever fine. Let's do this.

Q: *Write about a favorite family activity.*

Hands down,
surf fishing at Oak Island—
me, Dad, and Ty.
High tide at dusk, the cooler
filled with Dr Pepper and beer.
Chairs set up for when we want to plant
our rigs in the sand and take a break
from working the lines.
Next thing we do is read the beach—
look for sandbars and troughs, those spots
where the water drops deep.
The closest trough is where fish
show up for small prey—
crabs and sand fleas, for sure,
and the mullet you've put
on the hook for bait.

What we're hoping for—
bluefish, croaker, flounder, skate.
Some nights are lucky,
others not so much, but to be honest,
the best part is standing at the edge
of the water, the waves moving in,
then pulling back, the sky
going dark blue, almost black.

There's always a bonfire
burning further down the beach,
and from a distance, you could swear
the sparks were stars
just a little bit out of reach.

(That's pretty, right?
Just when you think
you know me,
turns out you don't.)

J
Jackson >
Sat, Sept 26, 12:34 PM

Keep me posted on the game

You could come

Nah

My mom's home for the weekend

She could come too

Yeah no

Whatcha gonna do then

You know to pass the time and all

Carolina plays at 3:00

ACC champs—gotta be

Clemson's tuff tho

Gotta go—Coach wants us there by 1:00

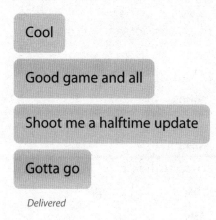

Cool

Good game and all

Shoot me a halftime update

Gotta go

Delivered

To: WBarth@childrenscounselingservices.com
From: StokesHP@ccs.k12.nc.us
Date: September 27, 8:12 PM
Subject: Re: Medical Note

Your research assistant?
How's *that* supposed to help?
What—I'm supposed to tell people
I'm not playing ball
because I'm doing a *psychological study*?

Dunno.
Maybe if I say I'm doing it for my dad.
Like, I say you're trying to figure out
how to help vets by talking to their kids.

Okay, whatever. Pretty weak,
but not as bad as people
thinking that I come here every week
because something's wrong.
Nothing's wrong with me, Doc.
I'm King of the World.

Haz

Attachment: WorkbookQuestion6.docx

Q: *Who are you most like in your family?*

Who cares?
I mean, what if I tell you
I'm most like my five-times-removed
great-grand second cousin?
That me and him
have a whole lot in common?
What's that gonna prove?

But hey: I got an idea.
I'll hand over some DNA
and you can run tests,
find out who my ancestors are.
Einstein, Mean Joe Greene,
Billy the Kid.
Could be anyone
smart, aggressive,
on the run from the law.
You tell me.

(Yeah, yeah.
Imma answer your question.
Next page and all that.)

Q: *Who are you most like in your family?*

Depends on how you mean it. Looks?
My mom, mostly—I've got light brown hair
and gray eyes, just like her.
Got my dad's size, but not his speed,
which sucks.
That's why I'm a safety,
not a wide receiver like he was.
Don't get me wrong—
I'm faster than most, not to mention
number one in Cumberland County,
but speed's not my main thing.

If you're talking about personality,
my dad—definitely.
We're both in charge, if you get me.
We don't follow, we lead.
We get impatient if you don't
do things right. Like, dude,
stand up straight, take the hit,
don't cry about it later.
And we're both funny as hell
and smart. Is that flexing?
Maybe, but it's no lie.
We've got parts of ourselves
we don't share, for sure.

Not everyone wants to spill
all their secrets to strangers.
Not everyone wants
the world to know their business.

To: BarthWB@childrenscounselingservices.com
From: StokesHP@ccs.k12.nc.us
Date: September 28, 7:15 PM
Subject: Re: Medical Note

Dear Dr. Barth:

My mom's cool with the "research assistant" idea.
She said she'll forward some emails
my dad sent from his last deployment
so I can do a "research project."
She said maybe for my "research project"
I could write how I feel about "what happened."
Not at football—she means to my dad.

Damn, it's like everybody I know
wants to give me homework.

Haz

P.S. Speaking of homework,
I did two more workbook questions.
Attached and all that.
You're welcome.

MP=Military Police

Attachment: WorkbookQuestions7-8.docx

Attachment: CrystalMosul.jpeg

Q: *Find a photograph of one of your parents when they were young and tell the story behind it.*

CrystalMosul.jpeg
Photograph: My Mom, Outside Mosul, Iraq

My mom, age nineteen, an MP
in combat boots & fatigues,
holds out a fistful of candy
to a bunch of kids standing
with their backs against
a mud-brick house.
They look at her from the corners
of their eyes, hands
tight by their sides,
faces nothing but frowns.
A bunch of US soldiers
just arrested their father
for making bombs,
& my mom just searched
their mother for hidden papers.
When I asked her what happened next,
my mom said the kids took
the candy & said *shukran*,
the Arabic word for *thanks*.

Everyone she met in Iraq
was polite, she said,
even the people who hated her.

Q: *Do you have siblings? Describe your relationship(s) with them. What would you say to them if you were being honest about your feelings?*

Describe my relationship
with my brother?
Dude, he's eleven.
You think we have a relationship?
What world are you living in?
I can tell you some things about him,
sure—like the kid picks his nose
when he thinks no one's looking,
and he's a little criminal,
always has been.
Last week I found comic books
in his backpack, each one still wrapped
in the plastic it was packaged in,
five copies of the same *Spider-Man*.
No receipt. There never is.
I told him I didn't get it,
and Ty just laughed. *What's to get?*
Said it felt good, like an itch
that got scratched each time
he stole something and then
gave it away to some kid
who thought he had everything.
Turns out, Ty said, *he didn't.*

Part two: What I would say to my brother.
Here's what I say to Ty
every damn morning:

Did you do your homework?
All of it? Cuz if you flunk math,
you don't play ball. Granny says
Mr. Barnhart called to complain
that in his PE class today you dropped
the f-bomb twice. Granny's not
gonna tell Mom, but could you
please watch your mouth?
Mom said you need
to text her at least once a day,
and don't forget to send
a message to Dad when you do.
In case you're wondering,
Whassup's not enough.
Make an actual effort, okay?
And buddy, clip your toenails
or at least put on some socks,
cuz that's just a whole lotta ugly
going on down there.
While you're at it, wash your hair,
cuz dude, your head *stinks*.
By the way, I saw the look on your face
when Granny said her checkbook

was missing. Put it back.
No one takes checks anymore anyway,
especially not from losers like you.
And you know about internet histories, right?
You're leaving a trail, idiot.
Fun fact: it's not really writing
a paper if you just copy stuff
off Wikipedia. Teachers check.
Get your act together. We've got
enough damage to deal with.
If I have to kick your butt to keep
you in line, I will. Count on it.

Sub in math

Cole just took over class

Dude—head for the exit!

Yeah cuz I'm not in enough trouble already

It's good for your rep

Jayda's been asking if you're ok since you're not playing

IDGI how is that good

Her eyes were all big like maybe she was thinking how she could make it all better

Still dunno if that's good

Could be worse

Maybe

Send it

Shut it

Delivered

To: BarthWB@childrenscounselingservices.com
From: StokesHP@ccs.k12.nc.us
Date: September 29, 8:23 PM
Subject: Re: Reflections on Monday's Session

Dear Dr. Barth:

You want me to reflect. Okay.
I reflect that you got a lot to say
about what you think I'm not saying.
But in spite of your so-called observations,
I'm not hiding a thing.
I told you what happened:
We played the Raiders.
I hit the receiver hard.
That's kinda the point of my position.
Like, I'm not gonna tap
the other guy on the shoulder.
*Um, excuse me? Could you please
stop running and give me the ball?*

Listen, what you've got to realize
is that Coach is just covering his butt.
That's it. What if that dude's parents
decided to sue because their precious baby fell down,
got a little bruised?
Only reason I'm here is so Coach can say

I got given some anger management advice.
Fair enough. I *am* angry.
It pisses me off that I'm missing games.
It pisses me off even more that you can't hardly play
real football anymore.
All those little snowflakes so afraid
of getting hurt. You wanna talk
about hurt? Ask my dad. Okay?
Just frigging ask my dad
what living in a world of hurt feels like
and then come back
and tell me I hit too hard.

Haz

To: BarthWB@childrenscounselingservices.com
From: StokesHP@ccs.k12.nc.us
Date: October 2, 7:30 AM
Subject: Email from My Dad to My Mom from Bagram Airfield,
  Afghanistan (EOM)

In case you didn't know,
FOB=Forward Operating Base
COP=Combat Outpost

Oh, and EOM=End of Message, even tho in this case it
wasn't

Haz

Attachment: Brandonemail1.docx

Brandonemail1.docx

To: crystalstokes@ncmail.com
From: bstokes@mail.mil
Date: January 26, 2015
Subject: Life at Bagram

Hey, Crys—

Someone should make a movie called Life in a B-Hut—part comedy, part tragedy. The tragedy would be the fact that you're living in a semi-private cubicle that gives you zero privacy. Or maybe that's the comedy. Is it better than living in a tent, the way we did in Iraq? Hard to say. I'm already feeling sort of claustrophobic—we're right up against the mountains, and you start feeling trapped after a while. Tell Haz to look up the Hindu Kush mountain range if he's looking for an extra-credit project. Does he still do that? Make up extra-credit projects that his teachers never give him extra credit for?

What everybody says about life at Bagram is true—aside from the occasional IDF, it's pretty chill, and the IDF attacks are all aimed at the airfield, so they're usually miles away anyway. I've heard some stories about a mortar landing next to a warehouse or something, but mostly they tell you not to worry about it. It's not like there's anything you can do one way or the other, right? Obviously you don't have to worry about IEDs inside the wire, but if you're out on Highway 1 (aka the Ring Road), watch out.

The Taliban owns the Ring Road. Not great news if part of your job is riding in a convoy to deliver goods to FOBs and COPs.

The internet connection has been crap lately. Tell the boys I'll try to Skype over the weekend, but there's no guarantee I'll get through.

Miss you/love you/love to my guys, Brandon

To: BarthWB@childrenscounselingservices.com
From: StokesHP@ccs.k12.nc.us
Date: October 2, 3:36 PM
Subject: Re: Email from My Dad to My Mom from Bagram Airfield,
  Afghanistan (EOM)

Dear Dr. Barth:

Oh, yeah: I forgot today's lesson
on the rudimentaries of military language.
Translated: I've attached some new vocab for you.
I hope you notice that I show you
how to use the words in a sentence.
That's called extra credit.
Don't forget to give me some.

Haz

Attachment: Vocab2.docx

Vocab Lesson for Dr. B: **IDF and IED**

IDF
Definition:

Noun. IDF stands for indirect fire, which is when you aim at a target without actually being able to see it.

Use in a sentence:

The IDF missile landed at my feet, so I ran away fast, except that there is no fast enough.
I should have taken those flying lessons
my mom wanted to sign me up for.
I should have been born a bird.

IED
Definition:

Noun. An improvised explosive device (IED) is a kind of homemade bomb. Mostly IEDs are planted by the side of the road or in the road. They are the main way US soldiers get killed in Afghanistan.

Use in a sentence:

The IED was planted by the side of the road like a flower that could kill you.

To: BarthWB@childrenscounselingservices.com
From: StokesHP@ccs.k12.nc.us
Date: October 2, 7:37 PM
Subject: Re: Your Reflection on Dad's Email

Dear Dr. Barth:

I reflect that I reflect so much these days
I'm turning into a mirror.
The fact is, I don't have that much to say
about my dad's email.
I mean, a lot of it I knew already
from stuff he said on Skype, right?
Not the IDFs or IEDs, I guess.
He never really talked
about that kind of stuff with us—
"us" meaning me and Ty.
So maybe that's why
when everything happened,
it came as kind of a shock.
It was news to me
that the situation was so dangerous.
My dad's not infantry, not a combat guy.
I guess that's why
I thought he was safe.
I reflect that maybe somebody could have warned me
that him getting blown up was a possibility.

Haz

To: BarthWB@childrenscounselingservices.com
From: StokesHP@ccs.k12.nc.us
Date: October 3, 11:24 AM
Subject: Email #2 from My Dad to My Mom from Bagram Airfield,
  Afghanistan

Dear Dr. Barth:

Attached: Dad email #2.
Vocab to follow.
Acronyms below.
(Yeah, I know some big words—
acronym's just one of 'em.
Onomatopoeia is another,
and don't even get me started on
honorificabilitudinitatibus.)

Haz

P.S. QRF=Quick Reaction Force. HNT=Host Nation
Truck. BAF=Bagram Airfield. BTW=By the Way.

Attachment: Brandonemail2.docx

To: crystalstokes@ncmail.com
From: bstokes@mail.mil
Date: March 21, 2015
Subject: Long Day in the Mines

Hey, Crys—

Sorry about not calling last night, but I've got a pretty good excuse. Yesterday I was in a convoy carrying a bunch of stuff—some trucks, some Class III petroleum, etc.—to the FOB in Ghazni and the truck a few trucks ahead of mine got hit. IED. At first I thought the truck that got hit was an HNT (we're not supposed to call them jingle trucks anymore, but it's hard not to when they're decked out like Christmas). Turned out that it was one of ours—a flatbed carrying two gunners and a truck. One of the gunners was hurt pretty bad and medevaced back to BAF.

After the dust cleared, we had to wait for a crane to load the truck onto another flatbed. So finally the truck gets loaded, and we're off. Thirty minutes later, we're going past this tiny village—I mean, it's nothing but a collection of mud and sticks—and all of a sudden there's harassing fire coming from three o'clock. "Not our mission, not our problem," right? The convoy commander reports the gunfire up to the battle-space owner so the QRF can get out there and handle it, and we take off. Same stuff, different day.

HAZARD   43

Anyway, it was supposed to be a twelve-hour mission that turned into twenty. And that's why I wasn't there to call, which totally bums me out.

Miss you/love you/love to my guys, Brandon

P.S. In case you're keeping score, I'd say the IED hit had a pucker factor of six. One day I'm going to be so chilled out, I'm going to bring it down to four, but it's hard not to take an IED situation personally when it's that close.

To: BarthWB@childrenscounselingservices.com
From: StokesHP@ccs.k12.nc.us
Date: October 4, 4:44 PM
Subject: Today's Vocabulary Lesson for Dr. B's Edification

Vocabulary: Pucker Factor

Definition:
Noun: How scared you are as measured by how tight
your butthole gets in a scary situation. The pucker
factor scale is 1 to 10, 10 being the most scared.

Use in a sentence:
I saw the copperhead snake sneaking under the deck
and stopped dead in my tracks—pucker factor 10, facts.
Granny's backyard is full of messed-up things:
blackberry brambles that'll suck the blood
from your veins, hornworms like tiny green monsters
on the tomato vines, the neighbor's pit bull
slamming against the chain-link fence.
But a copperhead, it'll mess you up
just to *think* about them pinpoint fangs
slipping like needles into your skin.
Granny says a copperhead ain't nothing
but a poison stick with a little bit of meanness mixed in.

To: BarthWB@childrenscounselingservices.com
From: StokesHP@ccs.k12.nc.us
Date: October 4, 12:16 PM
Subject: Re: Your Reflection on Dad's Email

Dear Dr. Barth:

My mom didn't tell us
about the convoy getting hit.
Her habit is to keep things
to herself.

I already know the next question:
How do you feel about that?
I feel like maybe she didn't want
to worry us.

Like maybe she thought
she didn't need to pass on
every
single
fact.

Haz

J
Jackson >
Sun, Oct 4, 2:15 PM

Sundays suck

What up

Homework

My moms on my butt
cuz my rooms not like
some magazine
or something

One good thing about living
with Granny—she Does Not Care

About anything?

Nah

She cares about homework and
like if we're eating enough

That's it

That's cool

Maybe I could move over there

Your moms food's so good tho

Worth the room hassle

Maybe

She says she wishes I was all
neat and tidy like you

My dad makes us do inspection

Sorta sucks

Made us do inspection

Yr dad'll be home
and on your butt in no time

No worries dude

No worries here dude

Delivered

To: BarthWB@childrenscounselingservices.com
From: StokesHP@ccs.k12.nc.us
Date: October 5, 7:18 PM
Subject: Today's Session

Dear Dr. Barth:

Attached is the email I talked about today—
the one from my dad last spring
where he explained to me and Ty how war works.
It's not like you think.
You could even say war sounds sort of boring.
So what?
What you do all day sounds sort of boring too—
sitting around on your butt
listening to kids complain.
You know why I don't complain?
Cuz I'm problem-free except for the fact
they make me see you every week.
Nothing personal, Doc. You're okay.
News flash: so am I, no matter what
anybody else says.

Haz

Attachment: DadEmail.docx

DadEmail.docx

To: StokesHP@ccs.k12.nc.us
From: bstokes@mail.mil
cc: StokesTR@ccs.k12.nc.us
Date: May 3, 2015
Subject: What We Do Here All Day

Hey, guys—

How's everything going? Things are good here. I'm a little tired, which is weird because not much happened today. Sometimes we deliver stuff to the combat outposts, and the guys there say their days are either totally boring or totally unhinged chaos. But life at Bagram is way different. A lot more routine, and there's almost always something to do, at least in my job. Unless there's a serious snafu down the line, which is what happened today. We were supposed to deliver some MRAPs (mine-resistant ambush-protected vehicles) to Fenty, near Jalalabad, but it didn't happen. Too boring to go into the details. The point is, I spent all day at the ready and then ended up doing nothing. Which wears you out in a weird way. You look back over your day and think, if I'd known I wasn't going to do anything, I would have done something. Gone to the gym, probably.

I've been thinking about what Ty said the other day when we Skyped, about how his friends don't get why I'm not over here shooting at people. Me and my buddy Rollie started talking about it, and he came up with a good way to explain things. So I thought I'd email you guys in case you could use this info in the future.

The thing is, being in a war is kind of like making a movie. Most of the people who make a movie aren't ever on-screen. I googled it, and here's just a short list of behind-the-scenes people who work on movies: producers, directors, the camera operators, the lighting technicians, the grips, the sound crew, the art director, the caterers, etc., etc. Hundreds of people, which is why movie credits go on forever. I could fill up three pages with all the people involved in making a movie who aren't actors.

War's like that too, the main difference being that if you're in the army, you get combat training whether you're headed for combat or not. My guess is that the camera operators don't have to take acting lessons (who knows, though—maybe they do). But even though everyone has to learn how to shoot a gun, only a fraction of soldiers who serve in war shoot guns as part of their job. The rest of us are behind the scenes. You've got your payroll clerks, your parachute riggers, bomber ground crews, drone pilots, weapons technicians, medical personnel, JAG guys (lawyers), on and on.

The movies make it look like war is all about combat. But without guys like me and Rollie delivering supplies—everything from trucks to tanks to water to food—to the COPs and the FOBs (combat outposts and forward operating bases), there is no combat. Without doctors and nurses, there's no medical care when soldiers get wounded in combat. Without ground crews and mechanics, combat planes don't fly or land. You get the picture.

I hope that helps explain it. Let me know if you have any questions.

Love, Dad

To: BarthWB@childrenscounselingservices.com
From: StokesHP@ccs.k12.nc.us
Date: October 8, 8:40 PM
Subject: Re: Reflections on Monday's Session

Dear Dr. Barth:

Monday was a long time ago,
but I'll do my best to remember.
Seems like we covered a lot of ground.
Seems like we made some big-time progress,
if you ask me—and who else you gonna ask?
Who knows me better than I do?

Haz

P.S.
Attached is the next Dad email,
which he wrote right before he came home
on vacation from the war.

P.P.S.
Let me pre-reflect for you,
save you the trouble of asking.
Here's the thing: sometimes
when I read my dad's emails,
I think he thinks I'm still a kid.

The last time I collected rocks,
I was eight. Why's he still
bringing that up? What's next?
Asking about my favorite bedtime stories?
If *Duck Dodgers* is still my favorite show?
I don't know why
it gets on my nerves,
but it does.

Attachment: Brandon3.docx

Brandon3.docx

To: crystalstokes@ncmail.com
From: bstokes@mail.mil
Date: June 16, 2015
Subject: Gone Shopping

Hey, Crys—

Fifteen days and I'll be home on leave—hard to believe it's
been almost six months. Anything you want me to pick up?
Yesterday me, Rollie, Sanders, and Garza went to the bazaar
that's right inside the wall. Garza's going home in a few weeks
and he wants presents for his wife and kids.

Most guys I know never leave BAF. You're not allowed to, for
one thing, unless you're on a mission. Besides, everything
you need is here, so even if you could go, there's not a lot
of reason you *would* go. But going to the bazaar feels a little
bit like getting away from things. I like seeing the people at
the bazaar—it's nice to see the kids, and you can get into
interesting discussions with the guys in the shops. I've pretty
much liked all the Afghans I've met. All the HNT drivers, if
they've got food, they offer it to you first and get offended if you
don't take some. Hospitality is a big deal here. It's cool.

Anyway, Garza picked up two cashmere scarves that looked
legit and toys for his kids. We drank tea with one of the shop

owners who's always talking about what it was like here before the Russians and Americans came in. Ate some kabob, which is the one thing I'll really miss when I go home.

I picked Haz up a rock that looked kind of interesting. The rocks here are a lot different from home, and some dude claims he found a ruby when he was at Camp Marmal up in Balkh Province.

Okay, that's it for now.

Love you/miss you/love to my guys, Brandon

To: BarthWB@childrenscounselingservices.com
From: StokesHP@ccs.k12.nc.us
Date: October 11, 10:52 AM
Subject: Interview Transcript

Dear Dr. Barth:

So, okay, I did the interview with Granny
like you asked. I guess
family history is kinda interesting.
Thanks for the tip
on transcription—it worked.
I just laid my phone on the table
and Google did the rest.
I thought about adding
some stuff to the doc later—
you know, so you could get
the real feel of the conversation.
I don't know how to put it,
but a person's voice tells you something—
like there's a music
in the way the words come out
that adds more meaning
to what's being said.
Never mind. I don't know what
I'm talking about.
And you wouldn't hear it anyway.

Haz

Attachment: GrannyInterview.docx

*Me and my brother Ty have been living with my granny, Wanda
Eaker, since my dad came back to the States in August for rehab
at Walter Reed Medical Center in Bethesda, MD, and my mom
went to stay with him. Granny's house is about three miles away
from our house, which no one is staying in right now. I did this
interview with her on Friday night.*

ME: I guess we could start by talking about you—I mean, your
biographical stuff. Like, how long you've lived here and all that.

GRANNY: I've lived in Fayetteville, North Carolina, my whole life.
This house—I guess it's going on thirty years. We moved here a
few years after your mom was born. The other day I accidentally
scraped my chair against the kitchen wall and I could see at least
five layers of paint from where the wall got scratched over the
years. When you got four kids, sometimes it's just easier to paint
over stains than try to scrub them out.

ME: Was my mom the only one of your kids to join the army?

GRANNY: Yeah, she was. Daniel talked about joining the Marines,
but he wasn't made for that kind of work—taking orders and
getting up every morning before the sun. He's the sort of person
who likes the idea of a thing better than he likes the thing itself.
Always been that way.

ME: What did you think of my dad when you first met him?

GRANNY: Brandon? I liked him well enough. He was fun-loving, which is a two-edged sword. Some people love fun too much.

ME: Did you think my dad was that way?

GRANNY: Maybe a little bit at first. But it didn't take long to see that he had a serious side too. He was good for Crystal. He understood her. Your mom—let's just say she wasn't always as responsible and clearheaded as she is now. She spent a lot of time in high school doing—well, another way to put it is that she was slow to mature. Anyway, Brandon was always encouraging Crys to, you know, work harder and take advantage of opportunities and all that. Got her to go to Fayetteville Tech after she got out of the service. He almost got her to go to a four-year college, but she got too busy with you kids and work and all that.

ME: Do you like having grandkids?

GRANNY: I sure hope so—I've got enough of them. But yeah, I do. Grandkids are easier than your own kids, that's for sure.

ME: Do you like having us staying with you while Mom's in Bethesda?

GRANNY: Now how am I supposed to answer that, Haz? You think

I'm going to say no? [laughs] Yeah, now that I'm used to it, I like having you. Tyler's a handful, but you do a good job with him.

ME: How did you feel about it when my mom went to Iraq?

GRANNY: I felt terrible about it! Awful! I sort of tried not to think about it, you know? I was real scared, and so was your granddad. Where she was, at that Camp—whatever it was called—

ME: Anaconda.

GRANNY: Yeah, that's it. That was a bad place to be. Dangerous. She had people close to her get killed by land mines. This one girl she was real close to got blown up by one of them explosive devices. That scared your mama to death. I mean, it broke her heart, but it scared her too. Me, I couldn't sleep after that, knowing Crystal could just walk outside and suddenly get blown sky-high. [Stops talking for a second] Oh, Haz, honey, I'm sorry!

ME: It's okay.

GRANNY: Well, I mean, it ain't news to you that it happens, now is it? You can be walking along or riding in a truck, and it happens. Your dad's lucky that . . . well.

ME: Yeah.

GRANNY: Anyway, I'm glad both of them's back. The government ought to stop that war right now. We ain't doing anybody any good over there. Too many people . . . well, just too many people getting hurt and for no good reason, that's my opinion. But I'm proud of your daddy and your mom, too. They did their duty, Haz. They had a job and they did it.

ME: Yeah, I guess so.

>>>>>>>>>>>>>>>>>>>>>>>>>>>>>>>>>>> [END OF RECORDING]

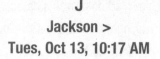

J
Jackson >
Tues, Oct 13, 10:17 AM

You got food?

Like did I bring lunch or what

I mean I AM STARVING over here

Also I really suck at math

It's all about the attitude

Mathatude

You sound like Mrs P

You can do football math

Why not real math?

Thats stats

Stats make sense

You can run angles=
geometry right?

Nah

Your mom cool

I'll tell her to make extra for tomorrow

Tell her to write me a mom note like she writes you with hearts and all

Yeah don't even go there

Already did

Delivered

To: BarthWB@childrenscounselingservices.com
From: StokesHP@ccs.k12.nc.us
Date: October 13, 12:14 PM
Subject: Workbook Homework Attached

Dear Dr. Barth:

Well, well, well,
if it ain't October 13.
That means in a week
I get to go back—right?
That's the deal we made.
Okay, it's the deal *I* made,
but you didn't say no.
By the way, I hope you're keeping track
about how I do the work
even when it's dumb
(which is most of the time).
In fact, attached is next week's homework
One week early.
I told you I came to play.

Haz

Attachment: WorkbookQuestions9-10.docx

Q: *Write about a time you or someone in your family went through a change—in personality, appearance, identity, etc.*

Q: *Write about a recent family event that impacted you. What did you notice at the time of the event? What details stay with you?*

Dude.
I know you didn't write the questions,
but you *did* assign the workbook.
The last time someone in my family
went through a change in appearance?
Dude. Really?
Recent family events?
You want me to write about *that*?
Then ask me your own self.
Use your own words.
Don't hide behind some stupid book.
Till then, I'll tell you some stuff
close enough to what you want.
But not that.

Q: *Write about a time you or someone in your family went through a change—in personality, appearance, identity, etc.*

He walked through the jetway
in his camo fatigues
and my mom stood still as a deer,
one that sees you coming
but hasn't decided when to run.
We didn't know if we should wait
until he made his way to us
or if we should cut through the crowd
that stood and clapped when they saw him,
like my dad was some
Fourth of July parade going past.

Thank you for your service,
everybody said, and I wished
they'd leave him the hell alone.
My dad coming home on leave
was none of their business.
When my mom found her voice,
she yelled, *Brandon! Over here!*
That's when everyone disappeared
and it was just us.

It turns out you can miss someone
and not know how much

until they come back—
until they pick you up,
even though you're almost the same size.
Until they say, *It's only been a minute, Haz.*
How'd you get so tall?

Q: *Write about a recent family event that impacted you. What did you notice at the time of the event? What details stay with you?*

The last time my dad came home on leave
was the first time I noticed the scar
on his fourth finger, right hand.
It was this skinny little white string
snaking around his knuckle.
Turns out it was from a fight in fifth grade
when some girl named Miranda cut him.
She brandished those scissors like a sword,
my dad said, and that made my mom laugh.
Look who's got a dictionary for a mouth!
That's how things worked with them,
I noticed, how she was always afraid
of seeming dumb and made fun
whenever he sounded smart.

The last time my dad came home on leave,
I noticed his bald shins when he wore shorts,
no socks, all the hair gone from years
of wearing combat boots,
the skin so white it was like part of him
had turned into a ghost.

The last time my dad came home on leave,
I noticed how he walked all around the house
when it was time for him to go back.
He stared at every photo on the wall
like he was studying for a test.
I noticed how he kept asking, *Remember*
that time we went to Ocracoke? Remember
when we drove to Atlanta to watch the Braves?
It was like he couldn't believe he used to live
like this—in a house, with us, the yard out front
covered in grass, not mines.

To: BarthWB@childrenscounselingservices.com
From: StokesHP@ccs.k12.nc.us
Date: October 15, 9:09 PM
Subject: Email from My Dad

Dear Dr. Barth:

Attached is the last email
from my dad, sent almost
exactly three months ago.
He came home a few weeks after that,
for reasons you already know.
My mom said she almost
didn't forward it.
But she wanted me to see
how much he was always
thinking about me and Ty.
You know what?
I knew that already.
I knew what kind of dad I had.

Don't know what kind I have now.

Haz

Attachment: Brandon4.docx

Brandon4.docx

To: crystalstokes@ncmail.com
From: bstokes@mail.mil
Date: July 21, 2015
Subject: Can't Sleep

Hey, Crys—

I'm wide-eyed awake and wondering what you guys are up
to right now. It's two in the morning here, so I bet Haz and Ty
are hanging out at the pool, and you're still at work. Man, I'm
glad you're back on the day shift—I hated the thought of you
working security at night, even if it was in an office.

So we got some bad news from the States. Last week Teddy
Colvert walked out to the woods with a gun and didn't come
back. Rollie got the email from Colvert's wife—she knew we'd
want to know. Nunez said maybe it was an accident, and
Rollie went off on him like you wouldn't believe. I mean yelling,
throwing punches, a total meltdown. It's not like Rollie and
Colvert were even all that close. But Nunez is young and green
and he needs to be taught the lesson that you can't wishful-
think this crap away. Colvert's been handling guns all his life
and did ranger training at Benning. Guys like him don't have
accidents with guns in the woods.

Rollie thinks Iraq finally caught up with Colvert. There was some bad business with a platoon leader that ended up with a bunch of dead civilians. Ugly, messed-up stuff. But I've known guys who didn't see much action at all go home and end it. All kinds of reasons why. For some guys, nothing makes sense anymore when they get home. I get that.

Anyway, I'm ready to come home. I think maybe it's time to get out, Crys. Four tours is enough. It's been a good life, and I'll miss parts of it a lot. But I've been way too lucky for way too long.

I keep thinking about how tall Haz is all of a sudden. I know he's still a kid, but just barely. Eighth grade means you're getting old. I've gotta get home and make sure him and Ty understand what's important in this life: Braves baseball, Clemson football, Carolina basketball, and Eastern-style pulled-pork barbecue.

Okay, don't worry about me when you read this. I'm good. I'm fine. I'll be home before you know it.

Miss you/love you/love to my guys, Brandon

To: BarthWB@childrenscounselingservices.com
From: StokesHP@ccs.k12.nc.us
Date: October 16, 7:33 AM
Subject: Fwd: Convoy Commander's Situation Report

Hey, Doc—

Here's the report they sent my mom.
It seems sort of flat, the way the army put it.
I guess you had to be there
if you wanted to really feel it.

Haz

P.S. SFC=Sgt. First Class (my dad's rank)

---------- Forwarded message ---------

To: crystalstokes@ncmail.com
From: Michael.White@us.army.mil.
Date: Tuesday, September 2, 2015, 11:02 AM
Subject: Convoy Commander's Situation Report

08-24-2015

A four-door Chevy Caprice blocked the road. The
convoy came to a halt. They waited. A young adult

Afghan male stood by the side of the road with a phone in his hand. SFC Stokes ordered the young man to drop the phone. The young man turned in SFC Stokes's direction but did not verbally respond. He did not drop the phone.

The IED explosion occurred at approximately 14:35. The blast came from under our second truck. According to witnesses, the air went black with dust and dirt, and chemical smoke filled their noses, burned their eyes. Pressure pushed against their ears.

The lead convoy truck flipped over. The blast beneath the second convoy truck caused it to lift into the air before landing and turning on its side. No fatalities. SFC Stokes, who was in the second truck, received blast injuries to his lower extremities and was medevaced back to BAF.

After the Airbus AS350 lifted, the dust settled. A flatbed arrived to haul the wreckage. An EOD team arrived to remove the Chevy. The convoy continued along its route.

To: BarthWB@childrenscounselingservices.com
From: StokesHP@ccs.k12.nc.us
Date: October 16, 4:23 PM
Subject: Re: Vocabulary

Look at you, asking for the vocab lesson.
Dude, I like your positive attitude
when it comes to getting schooled.

Vocabulary: EOD

Definition:
Noun. EOD stands for Explosive Ordnance Disposal,
which means getting rid of bombs and other explosives
from roads and fields and wherever they show up,
mostly by setting them off.

Use in a sentence:
The EOD team walked toward the bomb dressed like
astronauts, their robot out in front of them, one arm
waving in the air like it wanted to make friends.

To: BarthWB@childrenscounselingservices.com
From: StokesHP@ccs.k12.nc.us
Date: October 16, 8:14 PM
Subject: Re: Writing Prompt

Hey, Doc—

Below is my response to your prompt.
Gotta say it, dude:
I like the questions you ask
better than the ones they ask in the book.

Haz

The Way I See It in My Imagination

Granny says don't think about it
but how am I supposed to stop
A hundred times a day that truck goes up
like a rocket launched it
and a hundred times a day it drops
like the sky got tired and let go

To: BarthWB@childrenscounselingservices.com
From: StokesHP@ccs.k12.nc.us
Date: October 17, 9:15 PM
Subject: Re: Writing Prompt

Dear Dr. B:

You can send me all the prompts you want.
I'm suited up and ready to play.
Three more days, dude,
and I'm back on the field.
Right?

Haz

P.S. Thanks for what you said about my writing.
I don't really think about it much.
It just comes out faster when I write in lines, I guess.

To: BarthWB@childrenscounselingservices.com
From: StokesHP@ccs.k12.nc.us
Date: October 19, 12:31 PM
Subject: You've Got to Be Kidding Me

Dear Dr. B:

You talked to Coach? Coach *called* you?
Doesn't that violate our attorney-client privilege,
or whatever it is that we got between us?
He told me you couldn't tell him anything,
but you still listened to what he said.
How he was concerned about my "aggressive behavior"
even before I made that hit.
That me taking down that kid was the last straw
in some stack of straws he's been collecting.
So now Coach has a broken back.

Between you and me,
Coach is the kind of dude that overreacts.
But fine—at least I get to go to practice starting the 20th.
Monday afternoons are still yours—fine.
Just so long as we agree:
Once you give Coach a good report,
I'm back in the game.

Haz

You ready?

No need to ask

Nah, I know

Wish you could play in an actual game

Couple weeks maybe

Till then Jon's doing good

Not your level tho

Too much to ask dude

Yeah so true

You know that kid Foster

New 7th grade

Tight end

Dude it's only been a month

Not like my memory's gone

Yeah ok

Anyway, yesterday he was asking about you, like, were you actually dangerous or something

What'd you say

Not me, but Colin told him to watch his back

Dude I don't hit from behind

I take you on straight on

That's what I said

Don't worry, I told him you'll see him coming

Run run as fast as you can little man

Delivered

To: BarthWB@childrenscounselingservices.com
From: StokesHP@ccs.k12.nc.us
Date: October 21, 8:23 PM
Subject: Re: Checking in About Practice

Hey, Doc—

Yesterday I was like one of them guys
who's been a prisoner overseas—
like a hostage, right? Or a POW.
You ever seen a video of someone like that
when they get released and come back home—
how they get off the plane and run down the steps,
and when they hit the ground
they fall down and kiss it?
Today, that was me. That's right, Doc:
I kissed the damn field.
It felt good. Not as good as that time
I kissed Jayda Graham, but close.

Coach had the linebackers and safeties
do deflection drills, which was his way
of saying "Welcome home."
He knows they're my favorite.
It's all about tipping the ball out of the air
on its way to the intended receiver.
You give it a tap, let it fall,

and then pull it into your arms.
It's like rescuing something valuable
from a burning building.
You cradle that ball like a baby, Doc.
You carry it through the fire
& take it to some place safe.
Feels good.
Feels real good to be back.

Haz

P.S. Did my Monday homework assignments/prompts.
See? I ain't slacking off.

Attachment: FirstTimes.docx

The First Time Granny Took Me & Ty to Maryland to See
  Our Dad

We were scared
We didn't know what he would look like
We didn't know what we should look at
What about the parts of him that were missing
We didn't know how to look at what wasn't there

The First Night After Me & Ty Moved into Granny's
  House

Ty called top bunk & I let him have it.
I didn't care. It was just a bed.
Besides, the glow-in-the-dark stars
on the ceiling drove me crazy.
Whoever put them up there
didn't know crap about galaxies,
ours or anybody else's.

An hour after lights-out,
I still couldn't sleep.
The stars sort of shined

from the corners of the room.
You could tell they'd been there a long time.
Mostly the glow was gone
& they'd turned kinda green.

It was weird, like when you look
at the night sky & know
that some of the stars you see
aren't there anymore. I read how
the big ones can explode & blast
their chemicals into space.
It sounds dangerous, but it's not—
that's how baby stars get made.
Meteors, on the other hand,
can do some damage. They hurtle
toward the earth & sometimes
break open. Their bodies come apart.
The shards have a life of their own.

First Day Back to School After I Saw My Dad

There was a test in English on sentences
plus different kinds of clauses.
I studied in the car on Sunday,
on the way back from Bethesda,

which is where I saw my dad laid out
like a prizefighter down for the count,
blankets pulled up to his neck.
His mouth was mostly locked, it seemed like.
He hardly spoke two words in a row.
My mom was the one who did all the talking—
introduced the nurses and explained
each surgery, then sent us out of the room
when my dad needed privacy.

When I got to school, Mrs. Willow said
I didn't have to take the test
since I missed two days of class the week before.
But I was on it. I was *ready*—
ready to make a list of friggin'
coordinating conjunctions—
for and nor but so or yet—ready
to string together phrases and clauses,
tie words into sentences, all that crap.
Man, I was so ready
to make sense out of something.
Anything.

To: BarthWB@childrenscounselingservices.com
From: StokesHP@ccs.k12.nc.us
Date: October 23, 8:58 PM
Subject: Texts from Mom to Granny

I kinda wished I hadn't read these.
You really think this is a good direction
to go in?

PT=Physical Therapist
MATC=Military Advanced Training Center—basically,
it's where soldiers who lost arms and legs in the war get
physical therapy

Attachment: MomTexts.docx

*Texts from My Mother to My Grandmother from
   September 8 to October 9*

1. Tues, Sept 8, 9:44 AM
Brandon's pain is better today—they finally
found the right mix of meds. The nurse
is impressed with his bed mobility.
He can scoot up, sit on the edge, tho
I have to hold him so he won't topple
over. With just one leg, his center of
gravity has shifted.

2. Wed, Sept 9, 7:35 AM
The nurses say that every morning
he wakes up at 5:05 sharp. I checked
the report—that's when the truck
blew up (our time—2:35 p.m. theirs).
When he opens his eyes, he says his
leg hurts and points to the one
that's not there.

3. Mon, Sept 14, 4:49 PM
The pain's pretty much under control,
so the PT took him to the MATC
this morning. This stage is called

pre-prosthetic. PT says it's all
about "increasing muscle strength
and restoring patient locus of control."
That's how they talk around here.
I take notes all day on my phone.

4. Thurs, Sept 24, 1:34 PM
He likes it on the mats, likes to stretch
and work out. He likes being with
other guys in the same shape he is—
in fact, a lot of them are worse.
He likes the jokes, repeats them
over and over when he comes back
to the room. I laugh the first time,
but after that I don't.
To be honest, I'm not finding this
situation all that funny.

5. Tues, Sept 29, 5:15 PM
Visitors today—Brandon's folks again,
plus Matt and Jason. Some so-called
movie star I never heard of made
the rounds. Everyone talks about how
brave B is—and he is—but they
always sound like they're talking
about a child, not a full-grown man.

6. Fri, Oct 9, 11:11 AM

Waiting for the team consensus on
B's prosthetic prescription. He's
ready for a new leg, ready for
something to change. When he's on
the mats he's happy, but that's the
only time. I think he needs a psych
consult, but he's against it. Says he
doesn't want it. Says nothing's wrong
with his brain. But something's wrong.
I can feel it.

To: BarthWB@childrenscounselingservices.com
From: StokesHP@ccs.k12.nc.us
Date: October 28, 7:05 AM
Subject: Re: Reflections on Monday's Session

Hey, Doc—

It seems to me like sometimes
you get an idea in your head
and you can't shake it out.
Like, this week it was all about how you think
I'm "processing anger and grief" on the field.
We're all straight on the facts here, right?
My dad didn't die.
He got his leg blown off, which, okay, is bad.
But it didn't happen to me.
I got nothing to grieve.
Listen, compared to a bunch of people I know,
my troubles don't add up to much at all.
Like, in Mrs. Willow's homeroom class,
you can count the kids who still have dads
on five fingers of one hand and two on the other.
Some of the dads are gone for good,
and a few are gone for bad.
OxyContin keeps Cade's dad spinning
in and out of jail, MaKayla's too.
Jorges's dad died in Korengal,

and Tanesha's died outside Tal Afar.
Me? My dad's still here—
he's just lacking an appendage.
You think I'm angry about a lost leg?
You think every time I hit the field
I'm at a funeral for a femur?
Chill, Doc. You're overthinking this.
Yeah, I'm sad, but my dad
will be almost good as new in no time.
No harm, no foul, dude.
That's how we play in this neighborhood.

Haz

P.S. The reply to your "bonus" First Time prompt:
Attached.
Took you long enough to ask!

Attachment: Firsttimefootball.docx

The First Time I Played Football

Third grade. Pee Wee league.
At least that's the first time I played
in an organized way.
Me and Jackson have been throwing
the ball around since forever—
preschool, probably.
Man, I could not wait
for a real uniform, a helmet,
pads, cleats—not a costume,
but the real deal.
I was a Bengal—
our colors were orange and black.
I wore the shirt to bed,
slept with the helmet next to my head.

And I was good, even then.
I had good hands—like my dad.
I played wide receiver until I got bigger.
That's when I slowed down,
or when the other guys got fast.
But in third grade? Dude,
I was a speed demon.
Football was all I thought about—

I mean, I lived to play.

I even wrote a book about it.
Not my idea—we were doing a poetry unit
for school. To me, poetry wasn't anything
but a bunch of noise about flowers
and feelings and sunsets,
that sort of crap. But then my teacher said
we could write about stuff we liked to do
and see and think about.
Dude, I was set. Took a while to figure it out,
you know, find the right words and all that,
but once I did—like, once I learned the moves,
got a feel for how to play the game,
it was a cinch.

I called my book *The Bengals Win Again!*
Twelve poems about the most
amazing football team ever, according to me.
I ran like the wind into the end zone to score!
The crowd yelled for more!
I know, pretty dumb, but I was proud.
I even sent a copy to my dad in Afghanistan.
He sent a blue ribbon back with a letter that said
it was the best damn book that he'd ever read.

Dude that was a rough practice

I'm wiped

You gonna go to Kaylee's later

Dunno maybe

You going

Yeah for a minute

Bus leaves early in the morning

I hate morning games

Still wish I was playing tho

How about Jayda

She going tonite?

Prolly yeah

Can I hit you up for a ride

Yeah dad's driving so no dumb
questions so that's cool

Yeah always better when the
dads drive

For sure

How about Brandon

Driving I mean

Not tonight or anything

I guess

Dunno

You wanna eat here

Granny already cooked

Hit my line on your way over

yeah aite

Delivered

To: BarthWB@childrenscounselingservices.com
From: StokesHP@ccs.k12.nc.us
Date: October 30, 5:17 PM
Subject: Long Week

Hey, Doc—

Man, it's been a long week.
By the time I get back
from practice and do my homework,
I'm done. Fried.
I'm gonna do the interview
with my mom this weekend
since I still can't suit up
for a game or travel
with the team.
You & me will have lots to discuss
on Monday when I'm missing practice
to come spend time with you,
which is my favorite thing
in the world to do.

Haz

P.S. We got a home game against the Wolverines
on November 15. I'd sure like to show up & suit up.

To: BarthWB@childrenscounselingservices.com
From: StokesHP@ccs.k12.nc.us
Date: November 3, 7:04 AM
Subject: Re: Reflections on Monday's Session

Hey, Doc—

I'm still wondering about what you said
yesterday, about how sometimes
when something bad happens,
people absorb it into their bodies.
Their bodies take on the hurt
like a hit. That thing you said—
"the body doesn't forget"—
well, okay, maybe. I mean,
me, I've been thinking about how,
when I'm on the field working hard,
my body knows the play,
makes the moves, calls the shots.
It kinda feels like my body
has a mind of its own.
So now I'm wondering
if what you said yesterday
and what I just wrote
sort of meet in the middle somehow.
Well, I can't work it out right now.
It's too early in the morning to think.

But at least now you know
I actually listened
to something you said.
Probably just
a one-time thing, tho.
Don't get too used to it.

Haz

P.S. Attached: The transcript of my interview
with my mom, plus the weekend writing
I meant to send yesterday. Sorry for the delay.

Attachment: Transcript: InterviewwithmymomCrystalStokes.docx

I did this interview with my mom when she came home to Fayetteville for the weekend from Bethesda, MD, where she's staying near the Walter Reed Medical Center to be close to my dad. She comes down most weekends to see me and my brother Ty and to pick up stuff from our house that she or my dad might need.

ME: So how's Dad?

MOM: He's doing pretty good overall, I guess. They made a mold of the residual limb—it's the next step toward him getting a prosthetic leg.

ME: What's the residual limb?

MOM: You know—where his leg ends. I mean, the one that got—

ME: You mean the stump?

MOM: Yeah. I just—well, I don't like saying that.

ME: I feel you. Does he talk about what happened?

MOM: Not really. Not with me, anyway. He's started going to— I guess you'd call it a discussion group? You know, with other vets who were over there. They're, you know, processing their feelings about their experiences.

ME: You mean, like, therapy?

MOM: [Laughs] Yeah, that's what I mean. But lately with me, he's been talking about when we were both in Iraq. I think it's easier to talk about than more recent stuff. It's something we have in common.

ME: Do you think it was the same—I mean, being in Iraq and being in Afghanistan?

MOM: Well, I guess in one way, the army is the army anywhere, right? You're wearing the same uniform, working with people who are pretty much like the people you worked with in the States or wherever. You're eating the same food. I never went to Afghanistan, though, and I think Bagram is a lot different from Balad. A lot safer. I guess that's kinda ironic, huh?

ME: [Sort of laughs] Yeah.

MOM: The thing I was thinking about the other day is the way people joke around. Like in the hospital, there's amputee humor. A guy who got out a couple of weeks ago came back to show everybody his new tattoo. You know what it said?

ME: What?

MOM: "One Foot in the Grave." 'Cause, you know, he lost a foot to an IED. I remember when I was in Iraq, people made jokes about what scared them the most, like getting blown up or getting burned real bad. Everybody was scared about getting burned.

ME: Were there a lot of fires?

MOM: It was more if you got stuck in a Humvee or a tank that was on fire. So you would—I don't know, just experience your own death in a pretty terrible way. Anyway, why are we talking about this?

ME: Um, kinda weird, but we were actually talking about jokes.

MOM: Wow. Talk about going off-topic. But I guess you should expect your dad to tell a lot of dumb jokes about losing his leg when he gets home. "You can count on me, but only up to fifteen"—ha ha, so funny. Maybe it's a guy thing. Or it's just not my thing.

ME: So like, ten fingers and five toes?

MOM: You got it, Einstein.

ME: [Laughing] Pretty funny.

MOM: Yeah, I guess. I just don't get that kind of humor.

ME: So what's Dad going to do when he gets home? Will he still be in the army?

MOM: Actually, he was already talking about getting out before all this happened. But what he's going to do next, well, I don't know. Uncle Matt said your dad could help him run the landscaping business. So that's a possibility. Brandon could whip that business into shape in no time. Impose a little order.

ME: Dad's good at imposing order.

MOM: Well, logistics is what he does, right? It's looking at all the puzzle pieces and figuring out how to put them together so the trains run on time.

ME: Does that even make sense?

MOM: You know what I mean. If you need to get supplies delivered, and you got five trucks and eight locations in ten different states . . . okay, that don't add up, but you get the gist. Dad's good at that stuff.

ME: Moving on . . .

MOM: [Laughing] Please! Let's move on.

ME: So when can me and Ty go up to see him? It's been almost two months.

MOM: Yeah, well, I don't know. He's not in a great place, Haz. He's still working some stuff out, like I said.

ME: Wouldn't seeing me and Ty help? We'd cheer him up.

MOM: I think—how do I say this? I think—I don't think he wants to see you again right yet. He wants to be better before you come back up. Stronger. Back to his old self. He's not there yet.

ME: He wasn't doing that great the first time we saw him.

MOM Yeah, and I think he kind of hates that you saw him that way. And there's some other stuff he's working through, Haz. That's why this group he's going to is so good. It's helping him process what happened. Listen, I just need you guys to wait— maybe just a few weeks. At least until he gets his leg. At least until he's walking.

ME: I think it's messed up he don't want to see us.

MOM: Maybe it is. But it's a messed-up situation in general.

ME: It's Ty, right? He can't deal with Ty going up there and, I don't know, jamming the Coke machine—all the typical Ty crap. You need to get that kid under control.

MOM: It's not Ty, and don't tell me what I need to do. Ty is the least of my worries right now. The least of my problems.

ME: Which makes him my problem.

MOM: Granny can handle Ty.

ME: [Laughs]

MOM: You know what? Why don't we stop this interview for now? It's not going anywhere good.

>>>>>>>>>>>>>>>>>>>>>>>>>>>>>>> [END OF RECORDING]

To: BarthWB@childrenscounselingservices.com
From: StokesHP@ccs.k12.nc.us
Date: November 4, 6:49 AM
Subject: Re: Reflections on Mom's Interview

Hey, Doc—

You know what? I'm wiped. Plus,
I already told you I don't want to talk
about the fact that my dad doesn't want to see us.
What's to discuss? My feelings? Yeah—no.

Have I ever mentioned he played football too?
Wide receiver—fast, good hands.
If you'd ever seen my dad run, you'd understand
why he might appreciate it if we gave him
some time to get his moves back.
You got a kid, Doc? Let's say you do.
How would you feel if he had to see you undone?
I bet you'd want him to wait
until you were back to your old self,
all the pieces in place.
So I get it. My dad needs his space.
A wide receiver's job is to run his pass route
and stay open. He's an island of one—
no one's there to protect him.
So this thing my dad's going through?

It's what he was trained for.
He's got this
without us.

Haz

P.S. I did the research you wanted
on the prosthetic limb.
See attached and all that.

Attachment: GettingaProstheticLimb.docx

Before the process begins, the patient
gets asked a lot of questions.
Is there enough tissue left to cushion
the remaining bone? What's the condition of the skin
on the residual limb? Tender? Scarred?
Is the patient in pain?

It makes a difference whether you still have a knee,
if you have another leg,
if you're basically healthy.
You get a team to determine
if you're ready
to be fitted with a *socket that attaches the prosthetic*
to the rest of your body.
You'll get a *suspension system*
to keep one part hitched to the other.
Whether you get *sleeve suction*, *vacuum suspension*,
or *distal locking*, you might think,
from the sound of it,
that they're turning you
into a car.
Once you're fitted, there's still the part
where you learn
how to get around.
You could have problems with *hyperhidrosis*

(sweating a lot) or how the socket fits
if the residual limb shrinks or changes shape.
You might feel weak.
You might feel an ache
in the arm or leg that's not there.
That's known as *phantom pain*,
like your former limb's a ghost that won't leave
your body's house.

There's no information on how
the people who love you will feel
or the questions they might want to ask,

such as *How long and how much
will we miss the part of you that's gone?*

To: BarthWB@childrenscounselingservices.com
From: StokesHP@ccs.k12.nc.us
Date: November 10, 10:46 AM
Subject: Re: Missed Appointment

Done.
As in: I'm done.
As in: Leave me the hell alone.

To: BarthWB@childrenscounselingservices.com
From: StokesHP@ccs.k12.nc.us
Date: November 11, 2:46 PM
Subject: Re: Missed Appointment

I don't owe you an explanation.
Stop asking.
Still done.

To: BarthWB@childrenscounselingservices.com
From: StokesHP@ccs.k12.nc.us
Date: November 12, 1:14 PM
Subject: Re: Missed Appointment

The only reason I'm sending you this is to get you off
my back.

Attachment: Letter.docx

SUSPENSION OF STUDENT

November 6, 2015

To the Parent/Guardian of <u>Hazard P. Stokes</u>:

This is notification that your son/daughter, <u>Hazard</u>, has been suspended in accordance with North Carolina Statute 115C-390.5 for a period of up to five (5) days from <u>Monday, November 9,</u> to <u>Friday, November 13, 2015</u>. <u>Hazard</u> is being suspended because he/she:

Engaged in conduct that, under the supervision of a school authority, endangered the property, health, or safety of any employee or student of the school district in which the pupil is enrolled and that the student's suspension is reasonably justified.

Specifically, on Thursday, November 5, during a practice scrimmage, made an illegal tackle that resulted in teammate's broken wrist.

If you choose to appeal the suspension, you must communicate your appeal, in writing, to the District Administrator within five days following the commencement of the suspension as stated in board policy.

Students who have been suspended shall not be denied the opportunity to take any quarterly, semester, or grading period examinations missed during the suspension period or to complete coursework missed during the suspension period. Prior to reinstatement, school board policy requires that one or both parents/guardians accompany your child to school for a readmittance conference with the principal. If you have any questions regarding this matter, please call me.

Sincerely,
Elisha R. Mahomes
Principal
Cumberland Middle School

To: BarthWB@childrenscounselingservices.com
From: StokesHP@ccs.k12.nc.us
Date: November 12, 2:04 PM
Subject: Re: Missed Appointment

What does it mean?
What the hell do you think it means?
I'm off the team for the rest of the season.
Which is the reason
I'm not coming back to see you anymore.

To: BarthWB@childrenscounselingservices.com
From: StokesHP@ccs.k12.nc.us
Date: November 16, 8:20 PM
Subject: Re: Reflections on Monday's Session

Dear Dr. Barth:

I reflect that I'm back
because my mom is making me.
Hope that sheds some light
on the subject for you.

Haz

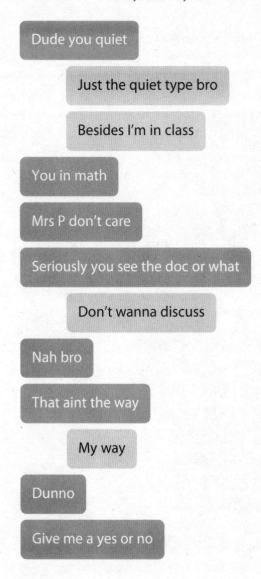

J
Jackson >
Tues, Nov 17, 10:44 AM

Dude you quiet

Just the quiet type bro

Besides I'm in class

You in math

Mrs P don't care

Seriously you see the doc or what

Don't wanna discuss

Nah bro

That aint the way

My way

Dunno

Give me a yes or no

Yeah I went

Whatever

Moms happy everybodys happy

That's the saying right

Yeah I guess

Good tho to talk

To talk stuff out

I guess

Didn't work the last time

Maybe it takes more time than that

I mean I dunno bro

Just haz you don't play dirty

You sure about that

Ask Tristan for his opinion

One time thing bro

Two time thing bro

You got food?

Always always

Joanie hit me up with some roast beef sammies today x2

J's my girl

Yeah she cool

meet up at the lockers

Yeah k

Delivered

To: BarthWB@childrenscounselingservices.com
From: StokesHP@ccs.k12.nc.us
Date: November 18, 7:43 PM
Subject: Re: Reflections on Monday's Session

Dear Dr. Barth:

Dude. Chill.
It's not your fault.
You say you thought
I was "making progress,"
that I was "exploring"
my feelings and "opening up,"
at least a little.
You're concerned
that you couldn't convince me
to take "ownership"
of my anger from the start.
Don't blame yourself.
It's on me, not you.
I am what I am, and it is what it is
till it ain't.

Haz

To: BarthWB@childrenscounselingservices.com
From: StokesHP@ccs.k12.nc.us
Date: November 23, 7:19 PM
Subject: Re: Reflections on Monday's Session

Hey, Doc—

I reflect that I'm wasting
everybody's time and money.
I reflect that I don't know
what to say. Today I saw
Tristan in the hallway,
his wrist in a cast,
arm in a sling.
I never had anything
against him. Dude's not
my best friend—especially
not now—but we got along
okay, you know? So, no,
I don't know what happened.
It wasn't me. I mean,
it was—I made the hit,
no getting around that.
But what happened right
at that moment—or a second
before—I'm not sure.
It's like something else

took over. That's what
happened the other time too.
I don't know how to describe it.
It's like my blood was filled
with teeth. That don't
make sense, but I can't
figure out how else to put it.
Everything was sharp and hot
and gnawing at me
and the only thing to do
was to hit something
as hard as I could so
I could break myself open
and shake the teeth out.

Haz

To: BarthWB@childrenscounselingservices.com
From: StokesHP@ccs.k12.nc.us
Date: November 28, 2:22 PM
Subject: Thanksgiving

Hey, Doc—

Hope you had a good Thanksgiving.
Me and Ty went to Mawmaw's house—
that's my dad's mom. She lives near Wilson,
about an hour away. Granny dropped us off.
She didn't stay—her and Mawmaw
never really took to each other, you could say.
Anyway, Mawmaw cried
as soon as she saw us, said my dad
would have been so proud of us.
She made it sound like he was dead.
(I texted my mom—he wasn't).
Mawmaw still lives in the house
where my dad grew up. Three bedrooms
for five kids back in the day.
And now, six cats. First thing
Ty said when he went inside was,
"Man, it smells like piss."
Nice. On that note, time to take a shower.
Writing attached.

Haz

Attachment: thanksgivingreport.docx

The Thanksgiving table was weighed down
with everything you'd want to eat—
roast turkey, yeast rolls, sweet potato casserole,
mashed potatoes, gravy, and seven kinds of pie.
All my uncles took their plates to the basement
to watch the game and dine in peace,
and for the first time ever, they invited me.
I know what you're gonna ask—
how'd I feel about that? Good, I guess.
But also? Kinda sad. Should've been my dad
offering the invitation, you know?
Anyway, during a commercial, Uncle Jason leans over,
tells me that when my dad was a kid,
he could memorize facts
like he had a camera behind his eyes.
Plus, he won a poetry prize once, my uncle said.
Don't tell him I told you. Even though
he's only got one foot,
he'd still kick my butt. For a minute,
I didn't know whether or not to laugh,
and then I laughed until I cried and couldn't stop.

To: BarthWB@childrenscounselingservices.com
From: StokesHP@ccs.k12.nc.us
Date: December 1, 4:14 PM
Subject: Re: Reflections on Monday's Session

Hey, Doc—

Until you brought it up, I hadn't thought
to count the days since I played.
Almost a month. Feels like I'm getting weak,
the way I hardly move anymore.
I'm asking for weights for Christmas
so I can stay in shape.
I might do lacrosse in the spring.
Never tried it before, but Jackson
says it's cool. I miss moving
across a field. I miss the way it feels
when practice is done and you've worn
yourself out. I miss using myself up.

But it scares me a little, like,
what if I can't stop making bad hits?
I used to play clean—no need to play dirty
when you're as good as me.
So what happened?
I don't know. Everything, I guess.
Remember the interview

I did with my mom, the one
where we were talking about jokes?
I keep thinking about people burning up
in their tanks. I keep thinking
about my dad and his leg—the one that's gone.
Where did it go?
Dude, where did it go?
I dream about war. A lot.

People think I'm violent,
but I'm not, at least I wasn't
before all this started.
You know that, right?
Put it this way—there's a difference
between playing defense and wanting
to put a hurt on someone.
There's a difference between
being a bulldozer and being
a tank. I never wanted
to break bodies. I just wanted
to push the bodies back.

Haz

To: BarthWB@childrenscounselingservices.com
From: StokesHP@ccs.k12.nc.us
Date: December 3, 7:44 AM
Subject: The Latest

Hey, Doc—

You know how my mom calls
every night at eight, right?
She's checking in to make sure we're all right
and give us the daily update.
Well, last night she goes down the list:
morning rounds, PT, how hard
Dad worked on the mats,
when he might come home,

and then she drops a bomb.

When my dad got blown up, she says,
a guy with a phone in his hand
was standing by the side of the road
where the convoy got blocked.
Maybe he was Taliban, maybe not.
My dad yelled at him to drop the phone—
Drop it! Drop it now!
—but the guy wouldn't do it.

As my mom talks, I can see it:

The gunner aims and waits—
the guy might just be a guy
watching what's going down,
but he might use that phone
to detonate an IED
that will blow them all sky-high.
My dad hesitates
and then he says,

Do it.

And the gun goes off.
And the guy goes down.
And the bomb goes off.
And my dad comes home

and sees it
and sees it
and sees it

Haz

To: BarthWB@childrenscounselingservices.com
From: StokesHP@ccs.k12.nc.us
Date: December 4, 5:27 PM
Subject: Text from My Dad—Screenshot

First text from my dad since he got back.

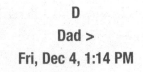

D
Dad >
Fri, Dec 4, 1:14 PM

Mom said she told you

Yeah, that must have sucked

Yeah, man, it did

It's good you're doing that group

Yeah

When can me and Ty come up?

Not yet

How about next week?

Dad?

Delivered

To: BarthWB@childrenscounselingservices.com
From: StokesHP@ccs.k12.nc.us
Date: December 6, 2:35 PM
Subject: Re: The Latest

Hey, Doc—

My mom says this is how my dad describes the group:
Seven guys in a circle who can't look
each other in the eye, seven guys who talk
to their knees as they describe
what they did or didn't do.

What they have is called a *moral injury*.
What they do is called *soul repair*.
I didn't know your soul could get broken.
I thought it was only hearts and bones.

Haz

To: BarthWB@childrenscounselingservices.com
From: StokesHP@ccs.k12.nc.us
Date: December 6, 8:32 PM
Subject: Re: Vocabulary

Hey, Doc—

My English teacher is always saying,
"We live at the level of our language."
Not sure I get what she's talking about,
but I think the two of you should go out,
maybe get married, have a couple of kids.
You're a friggin' match made in heaven,
the way you're both always going on about words
meaning something.

Definitions attached.
Aren't you tired of this stuff yet?

Haz

Attachment: Vocab3.docx

Vocabulary: **Moral Injury**

Definition:

> Noun. When you do something (or don't stop
> someone else from doing something) that strongly
> goes against your beliefs about what's right and wrong.
> Basically, it's when you or somebody else crosses a
> serious line and it hits you super hard emotionally/
> spiritually.

Use in a sentence:

> When the soldier shot the man on the road,
> it was like the bullet entered
> both of them at the same time.
> One bullet, two holes—
> a hole in the man,
> and a hole in the center
> of the person that
> the soldier used to be
> before he fired the gun.
>
> P.S. Just realized I didn't use the words, but you get
> what I'm saying, right?

Vocabulary: **Soul Repair**

Definition:

Noun. What you do to fix a moral injury—mostly through talking, and sometimes by listening. By talking about what you did and how you feel bad about it, even if it was something that had to be done. By someone else listening to your story and understanding what you're talking about because they've been there too.

Use in a sentence:

When you repair something
you fix the broken pieces or
replace a part that stopped
working and I guess
when you repair a soul
you're looking for a way
to sew it back up
so that a person's
spirit doesn't leak
out of their body like
water from a pipe

To: BarthWB@childrenscounselingservices.com
From: StokesHP@ccs.k12.nc.us
Date: December 11, 8:35 PM
Subject: Re: The Latest

Hey, Doc—

My dad called last night.
First time I heard his voice
since September—and back then
it was a croak of a word here,
a cough of a word there.
Now it's like he's breaking
open, broken open.
He said: *They're teaching me
how to get what's inside of me out.*
I told him I didn't think
he did anything wrong.
He was just doing his job.
Besides, it wasn't him
who shot the gun.
He said: *I gave the order,
I made the call.
But that's not the point.*
Then he said:
*I wrote something
I want you to read,*

so you'll know
how it felt
to do what I did.

What he wrote:
attached.

Haz

Attachment: letter.docx

To the guy with the phone:

I've gone over it in my head a thousand times. You standing
there with that phone in your hand, your finger pointed at the
screen. Maybe you were about to call someone to come get
you because the war was too close to where you stood, or
maybe someone you barely knew put the phone in your hand
and told you to punch in some number when the American
trucks came through.

Maybe you're the one who planted the IED and were about
to set it off. You might have gone to a Taliban school and got
recruited when you were thirteen, got taught how to shoot
guns and make bombs. How old are you, anyway? Twenty?
Older? I don't know. It was too hard to tell.

Whatever you were doing there, I had to make the call.

I wish I could ask you why you didn't drop the phone. You
looked right at me when I yelled. I know you understood. I am
almost positive you understood what I was telling you to do.
So you would have dropped it if you weren't up to something,
right? That's what I keep telling myself. You would have
dropped it and gone home to dinner—Kabuli palaw or korma

or kebab, rice and naan. You would have been thinking about how good the food would taste, how much you wanted to get away from whatever was going on.

That's what I keep telling myself.

Everyone says to me, "But you weren't the shooter. You didn't kill the guy." But I made the call. I gave the order to my gunner. And yeah, I've been trained for the situation. And yeah, I had to think about my guys. And yeah, there's a good reason to think I was right: I mean, an IED went off. That roadblock was a trap. You had a phone in your hand.

I saw you go down before I blew up. I don't know which part of that scene messed me up more. Justified or not, your death is on me. What I want you to know is this: I carry you with me wherever I go. Like a shadow. Like a ghost. Even if it had to be done, I still grieve it.

Brandon

To: BarthWB@childrenscounselingservices.com
From: StokesHP@ccs.k12.nc.us
Date: December 13, 8:37 PM
Subject: Re: Thoughts on Your Dad's Letter?

Hey, Doc—

My first thought?
If my dad comes home
carrying this stuff with him,
it lives with us, too.
I know: Deep, right?

My second thought:
If this guy's a ghost,
where's an exorcist?
If this guy's a shadow,
where's the sun?

I kinda thought if you confessed
what you did wrong, it went away—
like you were done with it and okay.

Reading my dad's letter made me think
that maybe what really happens
when you put your pain in the middle of the room
for everyone to see, well,

it doesn't go away, but maybe
it becomes another thing.
Another body you carry with you,
like a bird with one wing.
You bring it home and tend to it.
You're gentle with it.
You call it by its name.

But I'm not sure
it ever flies away.

Haz

To: BarthWB@childrenscounselingservices.com
From: StokesHP@ccs.k12.nc.us
Date: December 14, 7:14 PM
Subject: Re: Are You Okay?

Hey, Doc—

Yeah, I'm fine. Just thinking.
Like, what if I'd been that guy with the phone?
Let's say he was definitely there
to blow up the convoy—
let's say we knew that for a fact.
I'm trying to imagine what it's like
to be at war.
Like I'd been dropped into a video game
except it was real and the enemy
was against me and my family
plus everything we believed was true.
The guy with the phone?
He knew he might die and did
what he was trained to do.

I keep trying to get inside his head
but it's too hard to get outside of mine.

What I don't want to think about:
What if that guy with the phone was just a guy

on his way to somewhere else?
A guy who made the mistake
of stopping. Of wondering why
there was a car in the middle of the road.
Maybe he was thinking, *What are those idiot*
Americans gonna do about it?
Maybe he was thinking, *Man,*
I'm so tired of this friggin' war.

Maybe he was just thinking about how much
he wanted to go home.

Haz

To: BarthWB@childrenscounselingservices.com
From: StokesHP@ccs.k12.nc.us
Date: December 22, 7:18 PM
Subject: Re: How Was Your Trip?

Hey, Doc—

Me and Ty were at Walter Reed,
waiting in the hallway
for my dad's big entrance,
when this boy comes up to us,
wanting to know why we're there.
Our dad just got a new leg, Ty tells him.
The other one got blown off.
The kid puffs out his chest,
and says, real proud,
My dad lost both legs
and one of his eyes.
Like someone's giving a prize
to whoever's dad got it worse.
I'm all about competition, but dude,
that's one I was happy to lose.

Anyway, we shoot the bull with this kid
until my mom calls from the room,
You guys ready?
Like we're waiting for Santa Claus.

Weird. Even weirder, my dad walks out
the door looking exactly the way
he looked before. Skinnier, sure,
and pale, but he's wearing jeans
and you can't tell a thing
is different until he pulls up
his left pants leg, and there it is:
his prosthetic,
all shiny and robotic.
You think I should name it?
he asks with a grin,
and that kid—the one who was so proud
just a minute before—says,
You ought to call it "Lucky,"
and heads back down the hall.

Haz

To: BarthWB@childrenscounselingservices.com
From: StokesHP@ccs.k12.nc.us
Date: January 19, 4:50 PM
Subject: Re: Reflections on Yesterday's Session

Hey, Doc—

I reflect that I won't miss reflecting.
I reflect that it's going to be strange
to have Monday afternoons to myself,
at least for now. Lacrosse starts in a month.
I met with the coach this afternoon
to discuss my "issues."
I promised I'd come back
and talk to you if I started feeling
those feelings again. Who knows?
I might. Better to shed some light
on that stuff, amirite?
Better to talk it out
instead of letting it eat you up.

I saw Tristan at lunch today.
I told him I wished I could take back the hit.
He said it was okay, he understood.
Some days are just like that.
Besides, his wrist is fine.
I felt lucky all of a sudden—

that what I broke could mend, you know?
I could say I was sorry
and Tristan could say, *No worries, bro.*
My dad? He can't do that.
He has to live with the call he made.
The funny thing is, he did what he thought
he had to do. It was a decision, right?
Me, I wasn't thinking. I was just *doing.*
It's weird, but I wonder if that's kinda worse.
My dad made a choice.
I just made a hit.

Tristan wanted to know if I was going to play
in the fall. I want to, Doc.
I want to suit up, put on my pads,
hit the field, run the plays.
I'm good. I'm the best safety my age
in Cumberland County.
But when I think about the way it feels
to ram into someone, to push them down,
how it feels when our bodies hit the ground,
something in me—I don't know how to say it.
Sometimes you just get tired of war.

And yeah, I'll let you know how it goes
with my dad. I'm glad he's home,
but like I said yesterday,

it's not the same.
Hard to describe how he's changed—
it's the way he gets quiet in the middle of things.
The way he's always going out back to smoke,
even though he quit three years ago.

But last night at dinner he talked
about digging out the fishing rigs from the garage,
untangling the lines, getting them ready for spring.
You ever been to the beach in March?
Dude, the waves hit you hard
and the wind blows you down
like you're some little toy soldier
that can't fight back. But it still feels good
to stand at the edge of the water
and wonder what you'd find
if you could cross over
to the other side of that green field.

Haz

❖ ❖ ❖

Acknowledgments

A million thanks to my editor of over twenty years, the brilliant Caitlyn Dlouhy, who talked me through this, walked me through this, and encouraged me every step of the way. Thanks also to Carlo Péan for being ready with smart thoughts about every pass, and to my publisher, Justin Chanda, for his ongoing support and general awesomeness.

Thanks to all the Simon & Schuster sales reps who've done so much to get *Hazard* into the hands of readers. Thanks to designers Deb Sfetsios and Irene Metaxatos whose talent is evident on every page. Copy editor Clare McGlade continues to have my undying gratitude for helping me get both my facts and punctuation straight. I'm grateful to production editor Tatyana Rosalia for keeping *Hazard* on track from start to finish.

Many thanks to Col. Nicholas Lancaster (US Army, Ret.)

for his feedback on Brandon's emails. Any errors I made in rendering life at Bagram Airfield are my own.

I'm grateful to Carie Kempton and Tyler Beach for their insights on therapy and therapists, and to my neighbor Doug Williamson for introducing me to Brett Litz's work on moral injury. Again, any errors on these matters are mine and nobody else's.

The West Point Center for Oral History website (westpointoh.org) was enormously useful in my research when I was creating a backstory for Brandon Stokes. Thanks to all who developed this remarkable resource. Thanks also to Michael White—it was while listening to his oral history that I learned the invaluable phrase, "pucker factor."

To write *Hazard*, I read widely and deeply about the war in Iraq and Afghanistan. I read memoirs and fiction and poetry by soldiers, dug into the history of the war, and read multiple books and articles about the psychological, emotional, and spiritual impact of war on soldiers and their families. I owe a debt of gratitude in particular to the following writers: Elliot Ackerman, Stacy Bannerman, Graham Barnhart, Brian Castner, C. J. Chivers, Dexter Filkins, Matt Gallagher, D. A. Gray, Kirsten Holmstedt, Sebastian Junger, Phil Klay, Adele Levine, Brett Litz, Travis Mills, Kevin Powers, Virginia Robinson, Jonathan Shay, and Brian Turner. Thanks to the folks at The Wrath-Bearing Tree (wrath-bearingtree.com) for introducing me to so much fine writing by combat veterans.

Special thanks to my son Will Dowell, for sharing his

knowledge regarding all things football. Over the course of writing *Hazard*, I was constantly texting Will questions—*Which position plays meanest? What does a wide receiver do?* His replies were prompt, informative, and very helpful.

Thanks to Grace Meis for saving the day with her comic-book idea!

As always, I'm thankful for Clifton, Jack, and Travis the Dog Dowell for their ongoing support of my work, and for Kristin Esser, who always makes me feel like I'm up to something good. Thank you, Charlotte Vollins and Ellie Crews, for your long friendship and your passion for poetry.

This book is dedicated to Kate Daniels, who I first knew as my creative writing professor and who has remained dear to me and my family for over thirty-five years. I'm grateful for her poetry and her friendship. I met Sam Macdonald on the same day I met Kate; he's gone from us too soon, deeply mourned and sorely missed.

FRANCES O'ROARK DOWELL is the best-selling and critically acclaimed author of *Dovey Coe*, which won the Edgar Award and the William Allen White Award; *Where I'd Like to Be*; *The Secret Language of Girls* and its sequels, *The Kind of Friends We Used to Be* and *The Sound of Your Voice, Only Really Far Away*; *Chicken Boy*; *Shooting the Moon*, which was awarded the Christopher Award; the Phineas L. MacGuire series; *Falling In*; *The Second Life of Abigail Walker*, which received three starred reviews; *Anybody Shining*; *Ten Miles Past Normal*; *Trouble the Water*; the Sam the Man series; *The Class*; *How to Build a Story*; and, most recently, *Hazard*. She lives with her family in Durham, North Carolina. Connect with Frances online at FrancesDowell.com.